Rosebriar, England
1 3 3 9

It's the worst day of Juliet's life. For years
Marguerite, the young daughter of the
nobleman for whom Juliet's father works, has
been her best friend. But Marguerite is going
away, to be a lady-in-waiting at court, leaving
Juliet behind. A stranger on horseback has
stolen Marguerite's beautiful kerchief from
right under Juliet's eyes, and Juliet is afraid she
will be blamed for the theft. Worst of all, her
younger brother has accidentally released His
Lordship's most valuable falcon. Such an
offense puts Juliet's entire family in jeopardy,
unless she can retrieve the precious bird.
But how can a ten-year-old girl accomplish
what a skilled falconer spends years
learning to do?

GIRLHOOD
Journeys

Juliet

GIRLHOOD
Journeys

Juliet

A Dream Takes Flight
England, 1339

by Anna Kirwan

illustrated by
Lynne Marshall

GIRLHOOD JOURNEYS COLLECTION®

ALADDIN PAPERBACKS

For my daughter, Korena Elanor;
and for my nieces:
Carrie, Catherine, Alison, Wendy, Molly, and Jessica.

Grateful acknowledgment is made to Corbis—Bettmann Archive for the use of the illustration on page 68; and to Tate Gallery, London/Art Resource, NY for the use of the illustration on page 70.

First Aladdin Paperbacks edition October 1996
Copyright © 1996 by Girlhood Journeys, Inc.

Aladdin Paperbacks
An imprint of Simon & Schuster Children's Publishing Division
1230 Avenue of the Americas
New York, NY 10020

Designed by Wendy Letven Design
The text of this book is set in Garamond.

10 9 8 7 6 5 4 3 2 1

Also available in a Simon & Schuster Books for Young Readers hardcover edition.

The Library of Congress has cataloged the hardcover edition as follows:
Kirwan, Anna.
Juliet : a dream takes flight, England, 1339 / by Anna Kirwan ;
illustrated by Lynne Marshall.
p.   cm. (Girlhood Journeys)
"Girlhood Journeys Collection."
Summary: In fourteenth-century England, ten-year-old Juliet must recapture a valuable falcon accidentally released by her younger brother.
ISBN 0-689-81137-3
[1. Falconry—Fiction. 2. Middle Ages—Fiction. 3. England—Fiction.]
I. Marshall, Lynne, ill. II. Title. III. Series.
PZ7.K6395Ju   1996   [Fic]—dc20   96-2066

ISBN 0-689-80983-2 (Aladdin pbk.)

Reprinted by arrangement with Aladdin Paperbacks, an imprint of Simon & Schuster Children's Publishing Division.

C O N T E N T S

CHAPTER ONE

PREPARATIONS

"Princess Rosamund, fear not! Your brother the king was not poisoned," Juliet Blackwell said, trying to make her voice sound silvery. She held a pewter mug before her as if it were a great treasure. "He used this cup I made of unicorn's horn, so no poison could harm him."

Juliet's friend, Marguerite, promptly sat up in the chair where she had been pretending to faint with grief.

"Good fairy Lisette," she exclaimed, "happy was the day you came to this palace! No other princess has a lady-in-waiting who can do such magic!" Then, leaping up and hiding herself behind the tapestry wall-hanging, Marguerite changed characters, as she and Juliet did often when they played make-believe. "My curse on that too-helpful fairy," she muttered in the deep, raspy voice of Alsalabir, a wicked magician. "If she interferes again—"

Just then, a short, stout old lady in dark red brocade, Marguerite's nurse, Clotilde, bustled into the sunny room.

"How dare you make so free with your time this day?" she immediately began scolding. "Lady Marguerite, you are old enough to know better than to be playing like a child when your father and His Lordship the baron even now are on their way here for St. Michael's Day."

Juliet wished Nurse Clotilde would move aside from the doorway so she could duck out, but the plump woman's form filled the opening as completely as her complaints filled the room.

"Finish quickly with your day's sewing," she went on at Marguerite, ignoring Juliet completely. "You must help me oversee the preparations, for I cannot be everywhere at once. I expect that lout who's bringing the big chair up to His Lordship's chamber will make off with an ivory comb or a candlestick while my back is turned. You, child," she added to Juliet, finally acknowledging her presence, "get home to your mother, and don't keep Lady Marguerite from her duty. I never saw such idleness. And leave that cup on the table."

Without waiting for a reply, Nurse Clotilde bustled away as briskly as she'd appeared. Once she'd issued her orders, she expected to be obeyed.

"Never mind," said Juliet. "Maybe you can come see me later."

"She'll never let me go play today," Marguerite grumbled, dropping into a chair and picking up the embroidery she'd put down earlier. She pulled her needle out at arm's length to untangle her thread and started back to work. "If you hadn't brought the herbs for the cook and come up here to rescue me for a few moments, I wouldn't even have gotten this much time to do as I fancied. And it's not as if she ever lets me do anything interesting or important. With His Lordship coming for Michaelmas, and Papa, everything's got to be just so."

"Well, at least you'll get to see your papa," Juliet tried to console her. "And there will be feasting and music."

"Oh, yes. And if I say, 'Let's have apple pudding,' Nurse Clottie says, 'Fig cake.' And if I say, 'Let's have the pipers in from Warwick to play for the dancing,' she says, 'Old John with his lute always comes for Michaelmas.' So, what's the use? You know nothing unusual will happen. Nothing ever does at sleepy old Rosebriar. It won't be as if we were at court," Marguerite said, stabbing her needle through the colorful design she was working. "Oh dear, now look what I've done. This is supposed to be a picture of a shepherd and a lamb, and now the lamb is cross-eyed. I'll have to pick the last few stitches out."

Juliet looked at the embroidery and grinned.

"He does look foolish," she admitted. "But maybe you can just make his eye bigger."

"I wish my *life* were bigger," Marguerite muttered. "Why else would I still like playacting? I don't mean it's not fun. You do make up better stories than Harold the Rhymer. But I'm hardly a child anymore—I'm almost thirteen! Wouldn't it be fun to be a real lady-in-waiting for Queen Philippa? Why, she goes everywhere—France, Holland, Flanders—*every*where!"

"Like a bird," Juliet agreed.

"And we're just a couple of hens stuck in the dooryard." Marguerite rolled her eyes. "Pigs will fly before anything ever happens at Rosebriar."

Later, Juliet was sitting in her mother's herb garden, shooing sparrows away from the laundry spread on the hedge to dry. She was trying to play make-believe with dolls made of hollyhock flowers, but the game just wasn't fun alone. Juliet sighed and carefully propped the flowers against the pretend king's throne, a glittery pebble set on a carpet of moss. She wished Marguerite had been free to come play, but lately it seemed they both always had so many tasks. Time and again their games were cut short.

She stood and went to check the laundry.

Beyond the hedge, a serf was coaxing an ox to pull his cart out of a deep mud hole in the road. It was a good thing last night's rain had not come before the wheat harvest had been gathered, Juliet thought. Not only the autumn, but the Yule season would be merry at Rosebriar Manor and in its village. Mild weather meant harder work—a bigger crop to bring in—but then fewer people and animals would starve once winter came.

And the harvest work had certainly been long and hard this year. The whole village, every man, woman, and child, had been out in the fields as soon as the sky reddened each morning, even before the sun rose above the horizon. They had stayed there, reaping and raking and bending and lifting, till the moon was up.

That was why Juliet had been able to talk

Mum into allowing her to stay a little while at the manor this morning.

"Just for a bit," Joan Blackwell had said, combing a snarl out of her ten-year-old daughter's straw-colored hair. "Growing bones need rest, and children need some play. As long as your mind be not idle, I see no harm in it. But with St. Michael's feast day coming, we have too much to do for you to tarry long."

So, once her hair was braided, Juliet had hurried to do the milking and then had taken a basket of special greens and herbs to her grown-up brother, Tom, who worked in the manor kitchens. That was when she had run upstairs for the quick visit with Marguerite. When she'd returned, she'd had to wash and tend baby Eleanor, inspect her little brother, Alban, for ticks and lice, and feed the poultry and gather the eggs. Mum, meanwhile, had gotten all the laundry scrubbed by midday and gave it to her to hang out to dry.

The warm late September sun had already dried the thin cheesecloths. The aprons Juliet and her mother wore for everyday, though, were still damp. So were Father's and Tom's big shirts and Alban's little one, and most of Eleanor's things.

Everyone's thick stockings still felt as if they'd just come out of the wash tub.

One piece of laundry was spread out across its own bush. Juliet played her fingers through the fringe of the beautiful kerchief Marguerite had dropped near the gate last evening. It had been muddy when Tom found it this morning, so Mum had done it up with the family wash. Juliet had forgotten to mention it to Marguerite, but now she looked at it thoughtfully. It was as different from the rest of the laundry as a rose would have looked growing in a camomile patch.

It was not as if her own family had no pleasures, Juliet reminded herself as she admired the delicate fringe. After all, Father was a freeman, not a serf. He was forest bailiff of Rosebriar— caretaker of the woods and all the timber cut there—and gamekeeper for the huntsmen. Tom would be paid his season's wages, a whole stack of silver pennies plus a new shirt, on Michaelmas. And the garden herbs and sweet-smelling flower waters Mum sold brought in copper coins.

Juliet herself had a real silver coral-and-bells rattle Marguerite's family had given her when she was a baby, though nowadays she wore it on a ribbon around her neck. And when the family went out together on Sundays, Juliet and Mum always wore their alms-pouches containing a bit of money for the poor and lame begging by the church steps.

Marguerite was a real lady, though. In fact, as the only child of Sir Pepin D'Arsy, she would one day inherit his riches. Sir Pepin was the manager not only of Rosebriar, but of all Baron Hubert's sixteen other manors, as well as the twenty-three villages around them. No wonder Marguerite was so often lonely for her papa; he was almost always away at his duties. Since her mother had died four years ago, there was no one at the manor to watch over her carefully except crabby old Nurse Clotilde.

Juliet admired the fine cream-colored kerchief. She remembered the market fair last year when Marguerite had bought it. It had cost as much as Mum made all day selling herbs.

Juliet sighed again now and looked longingly in the direction of the manor. *Oh well,* she thought, *at least Wat Atwell has got his ox out of the mud.*

Just as she was about to gather up the cheesecloths and start folding them, she saw something that gave her good cheer. Piers Falconer's son was hurrying up the path from the side gate of the manor, the one near the mews, where the hunting falcons were kept. And he appeared to be coming directly toward the Blackwell garden.

Juliet dropped the cheesecloth and flung herself down on the patch of thyme where she'd been playing. She didn't know why she didn't want Gil Falconer to think she saw him coming and was waiting for him. She didn't know why being around Gil made her feel shy. He was just a boy. Just a nice boy. Really, his father's falcons were more interesting than he was. Except . . .

"Hullo, Juliet," Gil said.

Just a nice boy with a nice voice. But that was only because falconers couldn't be noisy, or they'd frighten their hawks.

"Hullo, Gil," Juliet replied. She waited for him to say why he had come, but he said nothing for a long moment. "Do you need more medicine herbs for the hawks?" Juliet finally asked.

"No," Gil said. Then there was another

silence, but not quite so long this time. "His Lordship's coming today. Father used that minty stuff your Mum gave him last week to get all the birds fit, so Sir Pepin and His Lordship can decide which of last year's birds to set free, and fly all the newer ones when they go hunting."

"All?" Juliet asked, suddenly excited, forgetting to be shy. "Agabus, too?"

Agabus was her favorite of all the birds Piers Falconer had ever trained to hunt. A young tercel peregrine, he was elegant: dark slate gray, with a white breast and flecked waist, and a wide crescent of black curving back from each piercing eye. It was no wonder Gil's father called him "a gentle falcon," just as if he were saying "a gentleman."

"Aye, Agabus, too," Gil nodded. "And look what I've been making for him."

Stepping around the end of the hedge and into the garden, he carefully loosened the pouch he wore on his belt. From it he drew out a fine little leather hood such as the hawks wore over their eyes except when they were having their daily exercise flight or being carried out before a hunt. The hood kept the bird from seeing anything that would scare or upset it.

"Red!" Juliet admired Gil's craft. "Where did you get red leather?"

"Sir Pepin lost one of his Spanish gloves, so he gave me the other one. And see, this feather tassel on top is from a green cockerel tail." Gil looked worried for a moment. "You don't think it's too gaudy, do you?"

"It's wonderful," Juliet said with feeling. "I mean, I think it will look wonderful on Agabus. I can't wait to see it on him."

"Oh!" Gil said, as if she'd startled him. "That's not really what I came for—I'm supposed to tell you to go to the mews. Lady Marguerite escaped from—that is, Nurse Clotilde—well, you're to meet Marguerite at the mews."

Juliet nodded and laughed.

"Nurse Clotilde never goes to the mews. She'll never find her there."

Gil grinned at her.

"A messenger came from Sir Pepin," he said. "Lady Marguerite seemed very excited. I shouldn't have kept you talking here."

"Oh, that's all right," Juliet said, suddenly shy again. "I mean, Marguerite won't mind."

A very nice boy, she was thinking. *With very nice eyes.*❖

THE MEWS

The mews was a little house about ten feet square, built to look like a miniature castle. Juliet always felt like a giant when she came near it. As she hurried across the grass now, she could just barely see Marguerite's eager face peering out of its narrow window.

"Juliet! Quick, before Nurse Clottie sees you!" Marguerite called softly.

As Juliet tugged open the door, several of the falcons leashed to the perches fluttered and beat their wings, turning their hooded heads from side to side to hear what was happening. Sometimes it seemed to Juliet that the saints who blessed the falcons and their keepers performed miracles every day, to keep such wild birds content to live indoors as captives, with their sharp eyes covered so much of the time. They could be trained for months, but they were never entirely tame. Yet, even when they flew free on a hunt, they almost always came back.

In the dim light, Juliet could see Marguerite bursting with excitement. Her gray eyes were dancing and her usually neat dark hair was a mess, with bits of feather clinging to her curls. Nurse Clotilde would have disapproved entirely.

"I just had to tell you the news," Marguerite said breathlessly. "You'll never believe it! It's as if Papa heard me wishing! Look!"

She held out a parchment letter with Sir Pepin's red sealing wax on its edge. Nurse Clotilde had taught Marguerite to read, and everything Marguerite had learned, she'd taught Juliet. Now Juliet could understand Sir Pepin's writing as well as her friend could.

"My dear child," she read aloud. *"I hope this finds you in good health. I plan to be home for Michaelmas. Be so good as to choose your warmest garments and your finest, and bid the servants pack them for a journey. Also, such pretty things as you are fond of, good threads and needles, your dear mother's prayer book, and the like—let them be put in a strong box fit for travel."*

As Juliet read, she felt her heart leap up into

her throat. Without her realizing it, her hand went to the little silver bells hanging on the ribbon at her throat—an old habit that comforted her when she was troubled.

"And bid Nurse Clotilde do the same for herself. I have such news for you, of a great change in your life, as I hope will give you cheer and contentment. But I think it best to say it when we are together. Your loving Father," she finished.

Marguerite going away from Rosebriar! It was the worst news possible. Nothing would ever be fun again without Marguerite.

But Marguerite was beside herself with joy.

"He's taking me to court, Juliet! I just know it! He's found someone who wants me as a lady-in-waiting! 'Warmest garments and finest'—that must mean we'll be somewhere exciting for the Christmas season! Isn't it thrilling?"

"Yes. It's wonderful," Juliet said, trying to be glad for her friend. Her thumb fidgeted with the silver bells; their jingling seemed to mock the idea of Yule at Rosebriar without Marguerite or jolly Sir Pepin, or even the familiar sight of Nurse Clotilde. "It's good news for you. No more boring old Rosebriar."

Juliet made an effort to smile. The little bells tinkled under her fingers.

"Everyone will just love you at court, Marguerite. Singers will make up ballads about you, and poets will write about your beauty." Juliet realized she was talking too fast, but she couldn't stop. "You'll be dressed in silk, eating from golden plates, journeying here and there for feasts and tournaments. I'll miss you, of course, but to be a lady-in-waiting—oh, it's wonderful. For you. . . ."

Marguerite put her hand on Juliet's shoulder.

"For you, too, Juliet," she said slowly. When she saw Marguerite's excitement had faded, Juliet felt guilty. "You're my dearest friend," Marguerite was saying. "Of course, you'll come and visit me. Why, you're like my sister. Say you'll come. What fun we'll have! Promise me."

"Of course," Juliet said. But she thought, *How can I? Father and Mum have no money to send me traveling. Besides, Marguerite feels I'm like a sister, but no one at court will think so. I'm a commoner. She's nobility. Being ladies-in-waiting was always make-believe for me. For Marguerite, it was just practice for the real thing.*

She had to change the subject.

"And you know who else will be going," she said, forcing herself to sound lighthearted. "Agabus!" She jingled her bells gaily. "Gil says he's ready to be flown by a hunting party, so he'll go to court with the baron, too, most likely."

The peregrine turned his face toward the sound of her bells and took several steps toward her. The short handling straps Gil called jesses, which falcons always wore, swayed, and the little Dutch bells tied above them on his legs tinkled.

"Juliet, please don't feel bad," Marguerite began softly. But Juliet hushed her with a wave of her hand. Picking up a feather from the sand-covered floor, she concentrated on Agabus. Quietly, she sang the first few notes of "Robin and Marion." A hunting hawk was trained to recognize some bit of song just as it would recognize the voice of its own chick, and this was the song Piers Falconer used to call Agabus.

And just as if Juliet were his mistress, Agabus sidled calmly along the long perch toward her voice, so that he was standing right next to her shoulder. Juliet gently stroked the feather she was holding around the edges of the jesses, across the tercel's yellow feet and frighteningly long black talons. And though he was not leashed in place and could have flown to another perch, he stayed by her, as peaceful and dignified as a statue.

"Juliet! He likes you!" Marguerite whispered in delight. "You're so brave! How did you know he'd do that?"

"Oh, Agabus is a dear," Juliet said airily. "I bring pigeons over a couple of mornings a week for the falcons to eat, so he knows me well. And Gil showed me how to get his attention with the bells and how to sing him to me." She frowned for a moment. "What's this?" She had noticed a shred of dry leather dangling at Agabus's shoulder. "That must be why Gil made him a new hood— this one's about worn out."

Juliet turned toward Marguerite and smiled again, a real smile this time. Marguerite had called her brave, and so she would be.

"And he *should* have nice things to go to court. You, too, Marguerite. I'll come over later and bring you some rosewater to wash your hair with, and some lavender buds to pack with your dresses, and peppermint in case you get a stomach ache from all the rich food you'll eat."

"And catnip in case I get a headache from all the music," Marguerite said with a laugh.

"And marjoram in case you catch a cold from all the princes kissing your hand," Juliet giggled.

"Oh, Juliet, I'm going to miss you so much!"

"Nonsense," Juliet said bravely. "I *will* come and visit. Somehow."

"Ju-lee-*ET*!" a small voice called outside the mews. "Ju-lee-*ET*! Let me in the birdhouse, too!" It was Alban, thumping with his little fist on the door. The best-trained falcons ignored the commotion, but a couple of small sparrowhawks screeched and beat their wings and started off the blocks they were sitting on, only to be caught short by the leashes that kept them from flying against the walls and window.

"Alban," Juliet whispered sharply as she opened the door, "you know better than to scare the birds! Piers won't ever let us come here if we upset them or if any of them gets hurt."

"I won't scare the birds," Alban said sweetly, trotting in on his plump little legs. "I'm a good boy, aye, Marguerite?"

"You're a darling, Alban," Marguerite assured him. "But you're such a big boy now, you frighten the hawks with your big noises. You're like a giant to them, you know. They can't see you."

"I *am* a giant," Alban growled, pleased at the

thought. "That's what I'm going to be when I grow up, a giant."

"Then be a quiet giant," Juliet told him. "And what are you doing, coming here by yourself?"

"You aren't in the garden," he informed her. "Mum wants you to bring in the dry clothes. She got a piggy to cook, and Eleanor knocked her pease porridge over, and Mum wants her clean apron. But you aren't in the garden."

"The laundry!" Juliet exclaimed. "I've got to go!" With that, she was out the door and a half-dozen running steps up the path before she thought to dash back for just long enough to say, "It's truly wonderful news, Marguerite. Don't mind my fussing. I really am happy for you. It's the most exciting thing that ever happened to us!"

Juliet and Marguerite had long ago discovered that the walking distance between the manor and the Blackwell cottage was as long as it took to eat one big apple. Running shortened the trip, but the muddy road made a slow run today.

At least, Juliet was thinking as she came nearer, Mum's apron might be dry by now.

But, what was this? A man on horseback was galloping into the village from the forest road. His

dark blue cloak billowed out behind him and, even
at this distance, Juliet could see
what looked like an
expression of fierce
determination on his
face. Right away, she
was curious. *What a
desperate fellow*, she
thought.

To her growing alarm,
he rode straight toward the
hedge around Mum's garden. Then, more
shocking still, he leaned over, reaching . . .
reaching . . . and snatched a piece of laundry!
It fluttered like a small white banner as he
wheeled his horse and took off back toward the
forest. He had stolen Marguerite's kerchief!

Juliet's first reaction was to run after him, to
keep him in sight even if she couldn't catch up.
His steed was powerful and fast, though—no dull
plow horse, but a rich man's mount. Juliet charged
past the garden, but just as the stranger reached
the woods, her long blue skirt tangled around her
legs and she fell—right into Wat Atwell's mud hole.

The stranger disappeared among the trees and
shadows. ❖

HELPING

Juliet couldn't believe what she'd seen. A thief! A robbery in broad daylight! And not by some poor, miserable soul trying to save himself from starving, either. That, she could have understood.

As bailiff, Father sometimes caught people hunting in the king's forest, or the baron's, or in the wooded park Marguerite had inherited from her mother. Most of the time, they had to appear before the court for breaking the law. But Juliet knew a secret: Marguerite and Sir Pepin had told Father he was to pretend not to know about any deer shot or firewood stolen by poor serfs in real need.

"I would do it, myself, Juliet," Marguerite had confessed defiantly. "I know it's wrong to steal. But if I had little children who were cold and hungry, and no neighbors or angels or good fairies brought us bread or alms, I would do it." She had sounded almost fierce when she said it last winter, when a widow and her four young ones were found starved and frozen to death in their hut on the outskirts of Rosebriar Village.

Now Juliet picked herself up angrily and tried to scrape some of the mud off her skirt. It was not fair that Marguerite's kerchief should be stolen, especially by someone rich enough to have a horse and cloak so fine.

The worst part is, it's my fault, she thought. *Mum put me in charge of the laundry. No one would steal our plain things, but I should have had the good sense not to leave Marguerite's scarf right by the road.*

Another thought struck her then, and she suddenly felt sick to her stomach. No one else had seen the stranger on horseback. Nurse Clotilde was always suspicious of anyone low-born. If Marguerite had mentioned where she had it last, Nurse Clottie might even think Juliet herself, or her family, had stolen the kerchief.

The Blackwell cottage was solid and well thatched, with room for two cows and four sheep in the shed end of it, as well as hens, ducks, geese, and doves. Mum's herbs hung in bunches from the rafters, so the sleep loft always held the scent of lavender and basil, which caused good dreams. Marguerite even said she preferred Juliet's cozy home to the cold stone manor house.

But today, Juliet knew the minute she entered the cottage that Mum was tired and out of sorts. Little Eleanor was sitting on the floor playing with two of Alban's tin toy horsemen. Mum was standing over the trestle table, punching and kneading a great mound of bread dough. Father's old ragged shirt was tied around her waist in place of her apron; the apron she'd been wearing this morning was now wadded up, wet with pea soup, in a basin near the water buckets.

"Juliet, where on earth have you been?" she said. "I've had need of you *and* my apron this whole hour, and you were nowhere to be found! I've no time to do any more washing, not with the feast day tomorrow. And look at you! Could you not keep yourself clean?"

At that, Juliet burst into tears.

Mum sighed, wiped the sticky dough off her hands on the old shirt, untied it and dropped it on top of the basin, then came around the table and put her arm around Juliet.

"Here, now," she said. "Juliet, what's the matter? Sit here on the hearth bench and tell your Mum what's wrong."

"I fell," Juliet wept, "and scraped my elbow and got all dirty. Because I was chasing a man on a horse, who stole Marguerite's scarf off our hedge. And what if Nurse Clotilde thinks I took it? But, oh, Mum, that's not the worst part. Marguerite's going away! She's going to be a lady-in-waiting and go off with Queen Philippa to Flanders and I'll never see her anymore, and she'll think I stole her kerchief because I envy her. And I *do*, I can't *help* it, but I'm really happy for her *too*, but I'll *miss* her, and I'd *never* take anything of hers. And that man on the horse looked like he was a *duke*, his cloak was so beautiful! And he just grabbed the nicest thing he saw and rode off with it into the east woods! What will I do?"

Mum took Juliet's hands and clasped them between her own, and held them warm in the lap of her skirt. "All these woes at once," she murmured. "What makes you think Marguerite is leaving?"

"She had a letter from her papa. I read it."

"And going to Flanders with Her Majesty?"

"Well, I don't know, I'm only guessing about that," Juliet admitted, sniffling and shuddering as she caught her breath after the storm of tears. "But she's going away."

"She has to go away, child. She is a lady. She has to marry well, for the sake of Rosebriar. Sir Pepin can't live forever, and there has to be a strong man in charge. Marguerite has to go where someone suitable will see her worth and ask Sir Pepin for her hand. That's her duty. You wouldn't want her to fail at it, would you?"

"No, no, of course not," Juliet said sadly. "She really wants to go away from here, too. We talk about it all the time. But we don't even know where she'll be going."

"You know Sir Pepin will arrange it well. He'll not harm his only child with a bad marriage. And Marguerite will come back to Rosebriar from time to time, I'm sure. This is her home. Her mama's buried in the church here, and her papa comes back as often as he may."

"But I'll miss her."

"We all will. But by and by, you'll also marry, and you won't have time for that."

"I'll *never* stop missing her," Juliet declared.

"What of this other tale?" Mum asked, gently

changing the subject. "Is this duke cut from the same imaginary cloth as the-queen-taking-Marguerite-to-Flanders?"

"I only said he *looked* like a duke," Juliet protested. "And he was certainly real."

"Well, it's very strange. But we'll tell Father to watch the east woods for outlaws. That's the road the baron and his party will be coming along from his manor at Ely. This fellow may be lying in wait to set on them.

"And, daughter—" Mum lay her work-rough hand on Juliet's cheek and looked searchingly into her brown eyes. "Your father is an honest Englishman, and your mother, too, is honest, and from a family as loyal and true as any in the kingdom. Sir Pepin knows this, and Nurse Clotilde does, too. Were it not so, she would not suffer you to be with Marguerite.

"Your brothers will not inherit a manor, and I'll leave you and Eleanor no jewels or treasure. But your inheritance is your honest heart and clever wits and your courage to work hard. So, thank heaven, you do not go without some advantage in the world. And, between us, we'll think of a way to repay Marguerite for her kerchief."

Juliet worked with Mum for a while then,

shaping the bread dough into fat loaves to make trenchers, big platelike slices to hold food, and small loaves to tear into bits and crumbs for thickening kettles of soup and pots of sauce. When they were finally baking in the oven in the kitchen-shed Tom had built out in the yard, Mum looked around and shook her head.

"That little knave Alban has not come back from the manor. Do go and find him for me, Juliet. There's my good girl."

"Can I take Marguerite a small jug of that rosewater I helped you make last week?" Juliet asked hopefully.

"There's a pleasant thought," Mum nodded, adding, "Take two, child, and give one to Nurse Clotilde. Perhaps that will sweeten her outlook."

Marguerite was in a storeroom when Juliet found her, selecting blankets and sheets for the maids to lay out for the guests who would be arriving.

"Oh, it smells heavenly," she said to Juliet,

breathing in the scent of the rosewater. "Nurse Clottie will be glad of it, with all this company."

Waiting for a good time to explain what had happened to the kerchief, Juliet was glad the conversation seemed to be taking its own course.

"It's already rather noisy down in the pantry and buttery," she told Marguerite. "I went to see if Alban was with Tom, and His Lordship's servants and carters are already arriving."

"I know. I wish I didn't have so much to do. When I was young, I used to like to listen to all their gossip about the other manors and life in the city and all."

Juliet had an idea.

"I can't stay long, but I have to go look for Alban in the great hall, anyway," she said. "Leave the rosewater here for now, and I'll help you carry this one batch of bedclothes. We'll pretend we're invisible, and we'll go see if we hear anything interesting between here and the sleeping chambers." *I'll tell her about her scarf later, when we're upstairs*, she told herself.

They each bundled up a great armful of linens and set out through the passageways of the big house.

At the first corner, Marguerite looked back to

Juliet and put her finger across her lips. They could hear voices around the corner in the next hallway.

"Thank the saints we're here," someone was saying. "Sir Pepin will feed us well at last. That Bogo de Dijon at Ely is as miserly as old King Henry. My stomach has been growling like a greyhound this whole month!"

Juliet buried her face in the sheets she was carrying to stifle a giggle.

Marguerite whispered, "Papa says the same thing about that Sir Bogo. Come on, they've gone the other way. We're still invisible."

At the end of the passage another hallway branched off toward the great dining hall, and a small spiral staircase led to the family chapel and bed chambers.

"Let's take these embroidered sheets to Papa's room, and then come back to the great hall," Marguerite suggested.

Juliet nodded and started up the stairs ahead of Marguerite. They had gone only a few steps up in the stone stairwell when voices carried down from above.

". . . D'Arsy's got a nice prize for 'is girl's what I say, if she's t'be married to the oldest of those four Gonfalons," a man was saying.

Then Nurse Clotilde's voice, sounding worried and angry: "She's hardly more than a child! She might at least go to some good convent until she's full grown. Betrothed at thirteen years old is one thing, married is another!"

"True enough. But, rich as 'e is, Lord Simon's got one foot in the grave—why, 'e must be fifty-four, and 'is feet swell up like bagpipes when 'e's sick with the gout. 'E won't want t'wait long t'see the next heir."

Juliet turned quickly, to see if Marguerite had heard, too.

Marguerite was as white as the sheets she had just dropped on the steps. She turned and fled. Juliet dropped her own armful and went after her.

Marguerite dodged two chambermaids and a page boy coming along the passageway from the great hall, then darted up the seven stairs that led to the solar room where she did her sewing. Juliet caught up with her there.

Marguerite's hand was pressed over her mouth as if to keep her from crying out.

"It can't be true, Marguerite!" Juliet blurted out. "You know it can't be true! Your papa would never—"

"Nurse Clottie thinks it's true!" Marguerite said. "She thinks I'm at least betrothed to that horrid old man! It's only *when* the . . . the marriage—"

"But your father's not that old himself!"

Marguerite's eyes were brimming over with misery.

"He's not as rich as Simon de Gonfalon, either!"

"You know him?" Juliet asked quickly.

"No, I've only heard of him. He's a friend of His Lordship's, a very important man. It *would* be good for Rosebriar to be joined with all his wealth! Maybe Papa thinks—"

"Nonsense!" Juliet stamped her foot. "He never would! Mum says—"

"I won't do it!" Marguerite said recklessly. "I'll run away first! I'll go live in the forest like Robin Hood! I'll . . ."

Juliet tried to think what Mum would say. It scared her to see Marguerite this way. And, to think—she'd been upset about her going as a lady-in-waiting!

"Marguerite, wait now. Think," she said. "You don't even know who that was, talking—"

"Yes, I do. Papa's new body servant he hired at Midsummer. *He would know the truth.*"❖

ESCAPE

Maybe it was a good thing, Juliet was thinking a quarter of an hour later, that Marguerite had been too shocked and angry to cry. It had turned out that the page boy they'd passed in the hallway had been coming to find her. The baron had arrived. Since Sir Pepin wasn't there yet, Marguerite had to go welcome him.

Juliet had squeezed her hand, then given her a hug. Marguerite was trembling, but her lips were pressed together sternly.

"I beg you, don't believe anything until you speak with your papa," Juliet had said in a low voice the page wouldn't hear. "My father would die before he'd let anything hurt us, and so would yours. There must be something here we don't understand yet."

Marguerite's gray eyes had looked dark and enormous.

"Maybe *you* don't understand, Juliet," she had said in a heavy voice. "Your life is simpler. People love you for who you are, not for what you own." She had turned and looked out the arched window at the late sunlight slanting over the fields. "I have to do what's good for Rosebriar."

Now, slipping in and out unnoticed among servants and strangers in the great hall, Juliet thought it was all terribly unfair. The trestle tables were already being set up for the supper to come. Clusters of the baron's knights and men-at-arms and squires stood about, in the way of the preparations, refreshing themselves from their journey with fragrant cups of herbed ale.

A number of ladies had arrived, too, wives, sisters, and daughters of His Lordship's officials.

An hour ago, Juliet would have loved to peep out from behind the hall's pillars at the flower-bright colors of their gowns, their fur-trimmed sleeves and trains, their tall, pointed hats like blossoms of foxglove and honeysuckle. Marguerite should be able to enjoy all this, Juliet's heart protested. She should not have to marry some man she didn't know, or be betrothed so long she'd have to go live in a convent that would keep her away from feasts and jests and music! She shouldn't have her own lovely kerchief taken by a stranger.

When Juliet had searched for Alban among all the hustle and bustle in the great hall, she realized he was not there. She began to worry. Where would he have gone?

She made her way out into the courtyard. Carriages and baggage carts clogged the area around the bake-house and granary. Elegant riding-palfreys and mules, even a company of the knights' massive war horses, were waiting to

be stabled. The place rang with shouts, whinnies, and laughter. Juliet was afraid she'd be trampled, and she grew more and more alarmed. Where was Alban?

Picking her way among the sloppy puddles all around the big stone watering troughs, she reached the wall of the kitchen garden and orchard. Just beyond the plum trees was the mews. Here, at last, among the lettuce beds, she found Alban. He was sitting on the gravel path, crying.

"Alban! Sweet pet, what's wrong, tell your Juliet!" she said, crouching beside him. She wiped his tear-streaked face with her apron.

"Oh, Juliet! I hadn't any bells like you have! And I couldn't remember the song! I *meant* to close the door, truly I did!"

"Alban," Juliet gasped, "you *didn't* go back to the mews!"

"Piers Falconer lets me. . . ."

"Hardly ever! Only when he's with you! Not alone! Did they tangle their leashes? They didn't hurt their wings! They didn't hurt *you*, did they? Tell me what happened!"

"Agabus . . ." Alban broke into a fresh flood of tears. "I tried . . . his hood was torn already,

Juliet, it wasn't my fault! I didn't know it would come off! I didn't know he'd fly away!"

Juliet stared at her little brother in horror. A missing bird was no light matter. A person judged guilty of stealing a trained falcon could be put to death. It was the law of the kingdom.

Terrified, she leapt up and searched the sky. Twilight was coming earlier these autumn weeks. There wasn't a bird in sight.

"How long ago?" she demanded.

"Just a little bit, truly. I was playing with my top under the currant bushes for a long time after you and Marguerite—"

"And did you see which way he flew? Did you watch?"

"Yes," Alban declared, braver now that he saw Juliet had no time to scold him. "He flew onto the wall over there. Then he flew up in circles, very high. Then he went that way." He pointed.

"The marsh," Juliet figured. "The river. Of course." Agabus was trained to hunt water birds.

She took a deep breath, her mind racing.

Agabus was a peregrine, meant to be the baron's gift from Sir Pepin, a costly gift. Surely, Sir Pepin would never think any of the Blackwells would steal from him—but even *losing* Agabus might mean that not only she and Alban, but also Gil, Father and Mum, Piers Falconer, perhaps even Marguerite, would pay dearly for their carelessness.

Unless she could find Agabus and bring him back to the mews, unharmed.

"Alban. Go home now. Go straight home. Tell Mum you're there, and tell her I have to do something else for Marguerite. Then play in the garden, or do some work for Mum, or something. But don't say anything about this. Don't lie," she added hastily. "Just wait till I get home to tell what happened. I'll be there as soon as I can."

She hurried Alban over to the gate onto the path home and watched to make sure he went, this time. Then she ran to the mews.

Alban's little wooden top and its long string lay abandoned on the ground outside. He had closed the door too late, she thought, but at least he'd closed it. Picking up the top, carefully, quietly, she pulled the door open and let herself in. Were all the other birds safe? She counted. There were the lanners, the merlins, the goshawks, and the fussy, savage little sparrowhawks. Only Agabus had been unleashed. Only Agabus was missing.

Looking around quickly at the low shelf with its boxes of training gear, Juliet found a leather glove that must have been Gil's. It was not big enough for an adult's hand, but it fit hers neatly and covered her forearm. There was a soft, sleevelike tube of cloth she'd seen Piers pull over a falcon to keep its wings closed around its body, but she didn't think she'd ever get it around Agabus. Instead, she fished out a hood that looked as if it'd fit, with good, strong ties. Then she found a leather pouch on a belt. She clasped it around her middle and stuffed Alban's telltale top and the hood into it. She couldn't find a spare leash anywhere, but there was no time to search for one. She would have to do the best she could.

Closing the door carefully behind her, Juliet noticed how low the sun was in the sky. It was hopeless, she thought, nervously fingering the bells at her throat. What new disasters could happen before this terrible day was over?

She looked around to make certain no one saw her go, and set out for the marsh.❖

THE MARSH

Where the river spilled out of the forest into the open land, it came first into a mysterious realm of reeds and feathery rushes. The ground under Juliet's wooden clogs was soft as pudding, and the water swirled slowly and pooled, lingering around green humps of weed jeweled with trapped air bubbles. Almost all the birds there seemed to have long, reedy legs or necks.

And almost all, Tom had told her, made good eating. That was why Piers always had some of his falcons and hawks especially trained to fly up over the marsh, watching, waiting on game.

It was late in the year, but the season had stayed warm so far. Juliet had not seen many wedges of birds flying south yet. The marsh was still a likely place for Agabus to find the sport his nature and his training required. But she was aware he might just as easily find another falcon, a passager, and join its autumn pilgrimage to Spain.

Looking up into the plum-pink sky, she could catch no glimpse of the peregrine. That did not surprise her, though, or cause her to give up hope yet. A gentle falcon, Gil had explained, always flew high enough that its prey didn't know it was circling above—until it was too late. Juliet knew what she had to do to discover whether Agabus was anywhere nearby. She had to rouse up some bird he'd want to strike.

And what if all her effort did not bring him back? *Better not think about that now,* she told herself. The light was fading too fast for her to stay long in the marsh. One chance was probably all she'd have.

She was standing on a flat pebble island about as big as two oxhides. Less than a bowshot away, across a shallow sidestream, was a stand of tall bullrushes where, Tom had told her, he'd once snared two cranes in one morning. *All right,* she thought, *perhaps something is in there now.*

Gathering her skirt up, she plunged into the stream, splashing and yelling.

"Hi-eye-EEE!" The water was far colder than

she expected, and her shriek at the shock of it had
fine results. Four big, sleek, ashen-gray herons and
a half-dozen ducks leapt up into the air, while a
good-sized animal—maybe an otter—slapped into
the stream off to the left.

The ducks flew off toward the stubble
of wheat fields in the distance, but the herons
beat their great wings and circled up
above the marsh. Their long legs
trailed behind them like
broomsticks, and when Juliet
saw their spear-like beaks,
she was almost as afraid that
Agabus would appear as she
was that he would not.

She staggered back to the pebble island,
straining her eyes to keep the herons in sight,
losing her grip on her skirt so it trailed unnoticed
in the water. How could such big birds fly so
swiftly, so high?

Then: a tiny speck upwind, even higher in the
red-violet heaven, but falling, plummeting, diving
more swiftly than anything, swift almost as an
arrow from Father's longbow—the peregrine tercel
Agabus had seen his target!

For a moment, the herons did not appear to

be aware of the danger above them. Then a commotion of crows further out in the reeds sent up the alarm, and two of the herons veered sharply off downwind. Juliet could see their black silhouettes against the sky, their beaks long as kitchen knives.

One of the other two swerved in front of its mate, dipping, then climbing again. Agabus seemed to have been aiming at the other bird, but for a moment, the dodging heron was flying right at him. The tercel raked his own long, tapered wings ever so slightly, and clipped the heron's wing with his talons as he passed. Juliet could see the leather jesses fluttering behind Agabus's legs. She could hear the bells he wore jangle from the blow, and saw heron feathers puff out from the stricken wing tip. The heron seemed to stagger in the air, then row its wings and turn, losing height, limping off into the darkening marshland.

Agabus had lost speed, but he righted himself in an instant and came on toward the heron he wanted. And this time, he struck farther up the wing. The heron whipped its head around to attack, but the damage was done. One wing was broken, snapped like a lance in a joust. With a hoarse croak, the heron fell into the weeds.

Fierce and joyous, Agabus followed.

Juliet kept her eye on where they came down. Heart pumping wildly from the thrill and fear of the battle she'd witnessed, she almost started to run toward the place. Common sense stopped her just in time. She must not startle Agabus now.

Taking a deep breath, she gathered her sodden skirt up between her legs and tucked it into her belt in front, so it bagged around her knees like loose breeches. Then, tinkling the bell toy with one hand, she waded carefully into the stream, singing as gently as a dove cooing.

"Robin loves me, Robin mine.
He would have me marry. . . ."

Agabus would know not to be afraid when he heard the familiar sounds. She pushed her way through the tough rushes, having to step carefully, toes up, to keep the ooze of mud from sucking her clogs off her feet.

Soon she could hear the uneven jingling of Agabus's leg bells not far away. She came upon him on a narrow spit of sand where the heron had fallen. It was dead already, though she saw no other wound on it but the bent wing at which Agabus was tearing. The fall must have finished it.

Agabus turned and looked coolly at her when

she came into the clearing, then went back to picking at the wing bone with his claws and curved beak.

Juliet could see that her bells would not fetch him this time; he already had food of his own choosing. Yet she hesitated to get much closer. If he flew now, all would be lost. It was almost dark. Even if he only went to roost in a willow, she'd never see him, let alone capture him and make her way back home.

She wished she'd had time to find a leash. If she could somehow get the hood over his eyes, he'd be meek. How did Piers recapture his hawks?

Suddenly she remembered—the stake with the long cord tied to it. And she *had* a long cord. Alban's top string!

Moving as smoothly as she could, continuing to sing so Agabus wouldn't get nervous, she pulled the pouch open and unwound the top. Then, bending down, still keeping an eye on the feeding bird, she tied one end of the string around a snag of dead branch half-buried in the silty ground about a yard away from the peregrine.

Agabus looked at her. Close up, unhooded, the yellow ring around his eye made him look shrewd, cautious.

Juliet tugged gently on the string to test it. It stayed fast to the branch, and the branch didn't move. She pulled the hood out of the pouch, and held it with her three outside fingers against the palm of the glove. Then, carrying the free end of the string, allowing its length to trail along the ground, she began slowly to circle around Agabus.

When she was standing opposite the branch with Agabus in the middle, she drew the string in close to the tercel's feet. Then she walked the rest of the way around. The string lay in a loop, partly across the dead heron's body, an inch or so from Agabus' talons. She watched as he took another beakfull of his prize, and while he stood still for a moment, she pulled the string taut and tickled it across his claws and in close to his legs.

He didn't seem to notice, any more than he had noticed the feather strokes she'd shown Marguerite. But now she had to move quickly. She tried to keep singing the same calm rhythm, but she found her breath catching as she walked the string around him another time.

When she was halfway around, Agabus looked up sharply. He did not try to raise a foot or take a step, but his wings suddenly shuddered slightly, as if he was shrugging. In a moment he'd raise them

and at least try to flutter off the ground. He
might actually realize he was being recaptured,
and take off. She couldn't let that happen. One
more time around with the string, as quickly as
she dared—and then she drew it tight all the way.

She had him.

He tried to take flight, but she held fast to the
string and he rose only a few feet, then thumped
back to the ground. He shook himself, then
relaxed and took another peck at the heron's wing.

What should she do next?

She must get him to sit on her gloved fist, but
she couldn't do that while he was wound up in the
string. She had to get hold of his jesses. And she
had to get the hood on him. Juliet felt as though
she needed another pair of hands.

First, she set the hood on the ground for the
moment, and seized the jesses in her right hand.
Then, holding her breath, she worked the string
loose with her gloved left hand so Agabus could
move his feet again. Would he pull free?

He only stretched his feet and shook them,
like a plowman taking off his boots after a day's
work. Juliet breathed a sigh of relief, thanking
heaven Piers had trained him so well. Then
she held her gloved fist right in front of him,

nudging his waist ever so slightly.

Just as if she were Piers Falconer, Agabus stepped onto the glove. He weighed surprisingly little for a creature his size. Juliet found she could balance him with little trouble.

Tucking the jesses behind her left thumb and looping them around, she reached for the hood. Looking Agabus in the eye for just a moment, she stroked his white bib feathers with the throat of the hood, as she'd seen Piers and Gil do a thousand times, then set the hood over Agabus's head.

She knew she'd never get the hood ties knotted one-handed. Piers would have used his teeth to help his clever fingers, but she didn't dare try that. She simply drew the ties as snug as she could, so Agabus couldn't toss his head and knock the hood off.

Somehow, then, with her free hand she bundled the heron into her apron and got the edge bunched over it and tucked into the belt. Herons made good eating for people as well as for falcons! Cautiously, she stood up. It would be an awkward, anxious trudge back to Rosebriar. But Juliet felt almost triumphant.

By now, the sky overhead was deep, magical blue. ❖

A NEW DRESS

By the time she was out of the marsh, the arm on which Juliet carried Agabus ached as if she'd been reaping wheat all day. But it was dark enough to take the short path to the manor, past the back of Mum's garden, without being seen. Part of her longed for Father to come out of the cottage and help her, but she told herself she must finish what she'd begun.

She did lean against the garden wall for a moment to rest her arm. And she managed to pull her apron and skirt loose from the belt and drop the heavy heron where she could get it later. Now she only had to get Agabus back to the mews without being seen.

It proved far simpler than she expected. Everyone at the manor, it seemed, was in the great hall at supper. She thought Piers and Gil must be

there, too. There was no sign they'd come to
check the mews and lock it for the night. The torn
hood still lay on the unraked sand under Agabus's
perch.

Agabus himself seemed drowsy after his flight,
conquest, and full meal. Juliet set him carefully
on his perch, then finally pulled her sweaty hand
out of the thick glove and gratefully let her arm
dangle at her side. With her fingertips, she dared
to stroke Agabus's silky back, and he let her do it.
If her eyes had not been getting used to the
darkness as she'd been walking, she would not
have been able to see him in the shadows, but she
could just make out his stately form. He was
beautiful, she thought, and noble—a gentle falcon.

And he had been free for a while. But now he
was captive again, ready to perform his duty for
his master, for the good of Rosebriar. *Like
Marguerite*, Juliet thought. *Like Sir Pepin. Like all
of us.* It was how the world worked, under heaven.

Still, he had been magnificent, swooping out
of the rose-colored sunset.

She put the glove, the pouch, the belt, and the
torn hood in the box on the shelf. She'd have to go
back to the marsh in daylight to retrieve Alban's
top and string. Carefully, she let herself out, closed

the door tight, and started for the manor gate.

Unexpectedly, a tall form stepped out of the orchard, carrying a lantern. By its light, Juliet recognized a blue cloak.

"You, there!" he said sharply. "What do you think you're doing here? Nothing good, I'd say."

"Me?" Juliet cried, outraged. *"Me?! You're* the one who ought to explain! *You're* the one who stole Marguerite's kerchief off our hedge! Fie! Fie on you, for shame! No one's kinder than Marguerite! I'm here because she lets me be here! *You're* the bold-faced thief, up to no good, stealing from honest folk!"

The young man in the blue cloak seemed speechless, but Juliet was exactly the opposite. All of the day's frustration and anger seemed to be boiling over, like an untended kettle.

"What could you be thinking, taking something that isn't yours! It's Marguerite's! And Mum washed it and rinsed it in lavender water so it'd smell pretty—because we *love* Marguerite, and what do *you* care! You just take what you want and ride off! And then come sneaking around the orchard as if it doesn't matter! Well, it *does* matter! It's wrong! Who do you think you are, doing such a thing?"

When she heard herself say those words, Juliet

suddenly realized what she was doing. She was scolding someone who was probably rich and powerful—powerful enough to have her put in chains for her words, not to mention for being in the mews at night.

She did not wait for him to answer. She turned and fled.

The stranger did not follow.

The cottage had never looked so dear and safe to her as it did when she arrived at last. It would have been a very small apple she could have eaten in the time that trip from the manor took her, but it was not short enough. She practically fell in through the doorway.

"Juliet!" Mum exclaimed. "Thank heaven, you're safe!"

"I was just about to go out looking for you," Father said, and indeed, he had the lantern lit and his cloak on. "Alban told us what happened."

"You said not to lie," Alban piped up. "I had to tell it, Juliet. . . ."

Juliet was suddenly so tired, she swayed where she stood. Father set the lantern down and picked her up as lightly as if she'd been Eleanor.

"Are you all right, child?" he asked, sitting on

the hearth bench with Juliet on
his lap.

"You're soaking wet,"
Mum said. "Get out of those
clothes. Wystan, here, get this
blanket around her."

"I have to tell you," Juliet
said, "I have to tell you the part
Alban didn't know. . . ." And
she told about Marguerite's betrothal; about the
fresh-killed heron out by the back wall of the
garden; about the thief in the manor orchard.
"And Agabus is safe," she finished, "but how can
I repay Marguerite for her kerchief?" Even as she
said it, her eyes kept closing.

"A heron," Mum said thoughtfully. "Herons
make good eating. As to that, maybe I have
an idea." She came over and stroked Juliet's
bedraggled, half-unbraided hair back from her
cheek. "You'd best sleep, daughter. And don't
worry. Sometimes things work out mysterious
well for good children."

Juliet did sleep—so well, when she awoke in
the morning, the sky was already sunny. Mum or
Tom must have milked the sheep already, she

realized. And the cottage was filled with a glorious aroma, of roast pork and herbs and . . .

"Heron," Tom told her cheerfully as she came down the ladder from the sleep loft. He was feeding Eleanor soppets of bread and milk. "Just the thing for a holy day feast for the D'Arsys and His Lordship, the baron! But look," he added, "it rather changed overnight!"

Indeed, Juliet could scarcely believe her eyes. The creation in front of Mum and Tom on the trestle table was as unlikely as it was gorgeous.

Partly, it was the roast suckling pig Mum had begun to prepare yesterday. And partly, it was the heron  Agabus had caught. The pig's head had been replaced by the heron's head and long, curving neck and great wings—the broken one patched back together somehow. The heron had been cleaned and roasted, too, and then pig and bird had been stitched together. The wing and tail feathers had been carefully put back in place, stuck into a spicy, golden glaze. The rest of the fabulous animal had been painted with shiny herb paste. It wore a crown of sugared mulberries and a garland of sugared rosebuds and crab apples.

"His Lordship's cook told me how to do this," Tom said proudly, "and Mum and I did it. It's called a 'cockentrice.'"

"You give that to little Marguerite," Father added from the hearth bench, "and perhaps it will make up for losing her kerchief."

"Oh, Tom! Oh, Mum!" was all Juliet could say in words. But she hugged her big brother and her mother, and that said the rest. Then she hugged her father, for good measure.

Mum just about had Juliet's hair combed when Alban came running in to say a stranger was coming up the path—and Marguerite and Sir Pepin were with him!

Juliet had been sitting there in her shift with her blanket around her. She looked wildly around and realized her stained blue dress was not where she had left it last night.

"You'd best hop to and give her that other surprise," Father said to Mum. To Juliet, he added, "It was going to be the great surprise for St. Michael's Day—before we had little girls turning into falconers and pigs growing wings, and the nobility visiting the bailiff's household.

But it's more like All Fools' Day here this morn
than Michaelmas! Surprises left and right! Look
what else your Mum made you while your back
was turned."

"Go, put it on quickly. Alban, get to the
bucket, wash your face." As she spoke, she reached
into the linen chest and pulled out something
folded, something rose-colored—a brand new
dress, Juliet's size. "I've been sewing it this whole
month. I was going to give it to you to wear to
church this morning. Here you go, over your
head. . . ."

By the time the D'Arsys and the stranger came
in the garden gate, Alban's face was glistening, and
Juliet was wearing the beautiful dress. She hoped
no one would notice she was barefoot under its
long skirt. Mum scooped up Eleanor from her
little chair and wiped the milk off her face with
the corner of the apron she'd just taken off.

"Sir Jerome de Gonfalon," Sir Pepin boomed
in his deep, jolly voice as the visitors entered the
Blackwells' cottage. "This is our bailiff of forests at
Rosebriar, Wystan Blackwell, yeoman—a good
fellow, Blackwell is, best we've got. And here's his
son Thomas—zounds, the lad's tall as a steeple
these days! Your age, more or less, Jerome, fifteen,

sixteen years old, something like that, eh? And Wystan's good wife, Joan, from the Blisse family, over at Alderhenge. . . ."

Juliet stared, astonished, then became aware Marguerite was trying to catch her eye. Over her arm, she was carrying her kerchief!

And why not? Sir Jerome de Gonfalon was the very man who had stolen it!

"And this," Sir Pepin was saying, with a twinkle in his eye, "this is my dear, late wife's namesake, Juliet. Whom, I understand, you have already had the pleasure of meeting."

Juliet felt herself blush. *What* was happening? Father was welcoming the guests, Mum was making a curtsy. Juliet followed her example, trying all the while to read Marguerite's lips. But Marguerite was trying too hard to be ladylike at the same time she was signalling Juliet, so it wasn't clear what she was trying to say.

". . . So it's good tidings this Michaelmas," Sir Pepin boomed on. "Sir Simon, Jerome's father, my great friend, and I have agreed, and the bishop will be here on Sunday to bless the betrothal of my dear Marguerite and this handsome young fellow! So I shall have a son at last—who is no bad shot with a longbow, himself, Blackwell, I might add. Well, Marguerite had to come and tell you all, first thing. . . ."

It was just at that point that baby Eleanor, thinking, perhaps, that no one was paying her sufficient heed, opened her tiny fist and hurled a soggy wad of bread she'd been hoarding right at Alban's nose, and the formal introductions turned into general conversation.

"May I call you 'Juliet,' as Marguerite does?" Sir Jerome asked courteously. Juliet nodded, still speechless. "I must apologize for the concern I caused you yesterday," he went on. "It was thoughtless of me—or, rather, my thoughts were all on His Lordship. You see, as we rode through the forest, his horse became somewhat unruly and carried him under a low branch. His eye was injured—bleeding—not too badly, thank heaven, but we did not know that then—and, the carts having gone ahead, we had nothing clean enough to bandage the wound. . . ."

Marguerite held out her scarf, and there, indeed, was a laundered but still visible blood stain.

"Sir Jerome told us how you informed him," she said, "that honesty counts for much here at Rosebriar." She spoke in a serious, courtly voice.

But she wiggled her eyebrows outrageously as she did it. "As my husband-to-be, he feels that when I go to stay with His Lordship the baron's household, where he has a position, and where I will reside in order that we may become better acquainted before we are wed in a few years . . ." The sentence was becoming very long, and Marguerite was clearly having difficulty keeping a straight face. "We discussed this over a game of chess last evening, an enjoyable match, which he graciously allowed me to win . . . though, not so graciously I didn't have to play my best to do it," she added under her breath, beginning to laugh. "He feels that, as I shall require a lady-in-waiting to be my companion and to assist me with all my responsibilities at court—well, in short, he suggested that anyone loyal enough to defend my interests, unarmed, before a stranger, on a dark night, ought to be our first choice. Will you ask your parents if you may come to court with us, Juliet?"

Juliet could hardly believe what she was hearing. But she could believe the happiness she felt.

"Oh, Marguerite," she said. "Of course, you know I will!"❖

<small>A F T E R W O R D</small>

JOURNEY TO 1339

The story of Juliet Blackwell is set in England in AD 1339. Juliet, her family and friends, and Rosebriar Manor and its village are made up, but they are based on historical fact.

During the Middle Ages, a typical community in Europe was made up of **feudal** classes—common people, church workers, nobles, and royalty—who were understood to owe each other loyalty and service.

The **peasant** farm workers were either **serfs** (sometimes called

A harvesting miniature from the Middle Ages

villeins) or free. Serfs were almost like slaves. They could not marry, move to a different place, or receive an education without permission from their **liege lord**, or master. They could not hold an official position, serve on a jury, or own a weapon.

Free people could make more choices for themselves about where they would live and how they would earn their living or improve their prospects with learning and travel. A freeman could be a legal witness or a juror; he might hold a local office or join the priesthood. He was required by law to own a weapon and to fight for his lord in time of war.

Serfs and free people alike all rented their fields and homes from the lord of the village where they lived. Everyone had to do a certain number of days' work for him each season, in addition to their work for their own families.

For his part, the lord owed the working people protection from enemy armies and outlaws, the upkeep of roads and markets for crops and goods they produced, fair judgment in their legal disagreements, and a certain number of celebrations and festive meals on holy days (holidays). In turn, every lord was a tenant and a **vassal**, or sworn supporter, of his own more

powerful overlord, all the
way up to the king himself.

During the fourteenth
century, life in the larger
manor houses reflected
the ideals of **chivalry**.
Romance tales and ballads
of the poet-singers known
as **troubadors** glowingly
described courtly behavior.
The **prowess** and honor of

**Chaucer at the Court of Edward III,
from the Tate Gallery, London**

nobles and knights were encouraged by the arts
and virtues their ladies cultivated.

Most tasks and pastimes kept men and
women separate from each other. One activity
often shared by men and women, though, was
falconry, or **hawking**—using trained birds of prey
to hunt.

During the Middle Ages, agriculture was a less
reliable source of food than it is today. People
counted on hunting for an important part of what
they ate. The strict laws of the Norman rulers
forbade anyone to hunt or gather wood in the
king's forests. But the smaller woodlands,
wetlands, and fields still offered game.

Dogs, hawks, and falcons were trained for the

hunt. The dogs sometimes wore leather armor and spiked collars to protect them from wild animals. The birds were outfitted with hoods, bells, identification tags, and **jesses** (leg straps). They had to know how to **bolt**, or fly at, quarry straight from the hunter's wrist; to **ring up**, or climb by flying in spirals; to **wait on** game, or circle in the air until the quarry appeared below; to **stoop**, or dive from a height; and to **bind to** prey—to catch and hold the quarry in the air. A falcon that had become used to humans was called **manned**. One that had been completely trained was said to be **made**.

Capturing and training a wild bird was difficult; some kinds of birds were rare and might even be imported from distant lands. A trained bird was therefore very valuable. Stealing one was seen as a disloyalty or insult to a member of the nobility. Even so, it is shocking to us, today, to realize that in medieval times, a person could be put to death for stealing another person's hawk.❖

ANNA KIRWAN has always been fascinated by
history. "When I was seven,"
she recalls, "my father showed me
a magazine photo of ancient
Roman horse armor that had been
discovered by archaeologists, and I
was hooked. The past is our
treasure. Knowing about other
times and places helps us imagine different ways to
enjoy our own lives."

  Anna has written poetry for adults and children, as
well as a medieval fantasy novel, *The Jewel of Life*.
She leads creative writing workshops for Amherst
Writers and Artists. The mother of a daughter and
two sons, she lives in Northampton, Massachusetts.

LYNNE MARSHALL was born and raised in South
Africa. She received her B.F.A. from the University
of the Witwatersrand, Johannesburg, in 1978. She
has worked as a freelance artist and illustrator and
has taught drawing and painting in her own art
studio. Her drawings and etchings have been
exhibited in galleries in major cities throughout
South Africa. In 1990 she moved to the United
States to further her education. She now works as
an illustrator and art teacher in Fairfield, Iowa.

Juliet *Circa 1339*

Marie *Circa 177?*

Kai *Circa 1440*

Shannon *Circa 188?*

Enter a whole new world of friendships and exciting adventures!

Share the adventures of the young women of Girlhood Journeys™ with beautifully detailed dolls and fine quality books. Authentically costumed, each doll is based on the enchanting character from the pages of the fascinating book that accompanies her.

- Join our collectors club and share the fun with other girls who love Girlhood Journeys.
- Enter the special Girlhood Journeys essay contest.
- For more information call 1-800-553-4886.

Ertl Collectibles

L I M I T E D

Actual size of doll is 14".

GET READY TO GO ON A JOURNEY!

Join our Collectors' Club and share the fun with other girls who love Girlhood Journeys.

We've created the Girlhood Journeys Collectors' Club especially for girls like you—
bright and full of fun, and always ready to travel.

Read about it...in your free issue of *Girlhood Journals*, the newsletter that features interesting articles
about *Girlhood Journeys* writers and artists, photos and stories from around the world, and excerpts from
forthcoming books.

Wear it...on your hat, jacket, or backpack. You will be in fashion with a *Girlhood Journeys* pin.

Write it down...in your *Girlhood Journeys* Journal. You can create your own stories and characters or
just jot down notes and ideas. We even give you a *Girlhood Journeys* pen!

Hang it...on your wall or place it on your desk. We're talking about a beautiful, signed, full-color
illustration created especially for Girlhood Journeys Collectors' Club members.

Okay so how do I join? Membership is available with your purchase of a *Girlhood Journeys* doll. Simply
look for the membership application form and information inside your *Girlhood Journeys* doll package.

YOU COULD WIN A *GIRLHOOD JOURNEYS* TRIP AND CHOOSE YOUR FAVORITE ADVENTURE!
Other great prizes too! See official rules below for complete details.

- Explore Kai's world on an African safari adventure.
- See the streets of Paris where Marie lived and danced on a special Paris holiday.
- Tour the castles and kingdoms of Juliet's time on a trip to London and the English countryside.

Or

- Ride the cable cars in San Francisco and visit Chinatown and Victorian sites where Shannon and her friends
once played.

HOW TO ENTER: Write your own *Girlhood Journeys* adventure story about your favorite *Girlhood Journeys* doll. The story should
be no longer than 500 words. Let your imagination run wild! The winner gets to choose the trip of her choice and have her story
published in the *Girlhood Journals* newsletter.

OFFICIAL RULES – No Purchase Necessary

1. HOW TO ENTER: To enter the *Girlhood Journeys Writing Contest*, type or print
on 8½"x 11" paper your name, address, age, daytime phone number (with area
code) and your original 500 word or less essay written about an adventure
taken by you and your favorite *Girlhood Journeys* doll. Mail your entry to:
Girlhood Journeys Writing Contest, P.O. Box 8947, St. Louis, MO 63101. All
entries must be received by December 31, 1997. The Ertl Company, Inc., is not
responsible for late, lost, damaged, misdirected or postage-due mail. Illegible
or incomplete entries will be disqualified. Only one entry per entrant. Entries
must be original and not previously published in any medium. All entries
become the property of The Ertl Company, Inc., and will not be returned.
Winner must sign a release signing all rights to The Ertl Company, Inc.

2. JUDGING: The winners will be selected by an independent judging panel,
whose decisions are final on all matters related to this contest, on or about
January 31, 1998. Winners will be selected based on originality/creativity,
writing skill, and appropriateness, in equal value. Only one prize per
household or family. All prizes will be awarded.

3. NOTIFICATION: The Grand Prize winner will be notified by mail on or
about February 15, 1998. Prize will be awarded in name of winner's parent or
guardian who will be required to sign and return an affidavit of eligibility and
liability and publicity release within 14 days of notification. Grand prize
winner's travel companion must also sign a publicity/liability release and
return it within the same time period. Travel companion must be 18 years or
over or traveling with a parent or guardian. In the event of noncompliance
within this time period, prize will be forfeited and an alternate winner will be
selected. Any prize notification or prize returned to the sponsor or its agencies
as undeliverable will result in disqualification and the awarding of that prize
to an alternate winner. Acceptance of prize offered constitutes permission to

use winner's name, biographical information and/or likeness for purposes of
advertising and promotion without notice or further compensation as
permitted by law.

4. ELIGIBILITY: Contest is open to residents of the United Sates who are 6-13
years of age. Employees and the immediate families of employees of The Ertl
Company, Inc., its affiliates, subsidiaries, advertising and promotion agencies,
and all retail licensees are ineligible. This contest is void where prohibited by
law, and is subject to federal, state, and local regulations. Taxes on prizes, if any,
are the responsibility of individual winners. By participating in this contest,
participants agree to be bound by all Official Rules of this contest.

5. PRIZE DETAILS: Grand Prize (1): Trip for winner and one (1) guest to ONE
of the following destinations: Trip Choice One • Paris, Chateaux and
Countryside Holiday (9 nights); Trip Choice Two • African Safari Adventure
(12 nights); Trip Choice Three • London and English Countryside (9 nights);
Trip Choice Four • Victorian San Francisco (6 nights). Each trip for two (2)
includes round-trip coach airfare (to/from the gateway city nearest the
winner's home), double-occupancy accommodations, and a guided tour or
safari. Travel must be taken by February 18, 1999. Estimated retail value of each
trip for 2: $2,800.00–$9,270.00 based on destination selected and departure city.
Meals, gratuities, and all other expenses not specified herein are winner's
responsibility. First Prize (4): Gift set of the entire *Girlhood Journeys* book series
published by Simon & Schuster. Estimated retail value: $23.95 each. Total
estimated retail value of all prizes: $2,895.80–$9,365.80. Winners may not
substitute or transfer prizes but sponsor reserves the right to substitute prizes
with prizes of equal or greater value, if advertised prize becomes unavailable.

6. WINNERS' LIST: For a winners' list, send a self-addressed, stamped
envelope by March 1, 1998 to: Girlhood Journeys Writing Contest Winners, P.O.
Box 8980, St. Louis, MO 63101.